Frances Forbes Robertson

The Devil's Pronoun

And Other Phantasies

Frances Forbes Robertson

The Devil's Pronoun
And Other Phantasies

ISBN/EAN: 9783743443990

Manufactured in Europe, USA, Canada, Australia, Japa

Cover: Foto ©Andreas Hilbeck / pixelio.de

Manufactured and distributed by brebook publishing software
(www.brebook.com)

Frances Forbes Robertson

The Devil's Pronoun

THE DEVIL'S PRONOUN
AND OTHER PHANTASIES

THE DEVIL'S PRONOUN AND OTHER PHANTASIES

By FRANCES FORBES ROBERTSON

WITH FIVE DESIGNS BY E. F. R.

REEVES & TURNER
5 WELLINGTON STREET
STRAND LONDON 1894

To the

REVEREND ROBERT FRANCIS CLARKE

Priest and Sage

I humbly dedicate this little book,

in respect and affection, without his permission

F. F. R.

CONTENTS

THE DEVIL'S PRONOUN

THE DEVIL'S PRONOUN

A Legend

" *For ye have eaten up the vineyard ; the spoil of the poor is in your houses.*"

" *What mean ye that ye beat my people to pieces, and grind the faces of the poor ?* "

ISAIAH iii.

THERE was an Island lovely from sea-boundary to sea-boundary, rich in all such produce as was needful to man.

Those who dwelt there were a race of

fair and happy people, tilling the soil and living in peaceful commune.

They had no king nor master, nor indeed were they governed or ruled by any, unless perhaps by a certain charming sway of childhood's power.

They spoke a language which radically differed from all others in the peculiar absence of the possessive pronoun, and some strange customs were practised which, doubtless, to the uninitiated, would seem very odd. There were no prison-houses, courts of law, money-exchange, nor laboratories for the cutting up of live creatures ; neither had they communication with the world beyond the seas.

"Parents, respect the little children," seemed to be the basis of their moral code : all was understood when this saying was pronounced ; and, if one may judge by the universal practice of virtue, the maxim was not only admirable, but all-sufficing.

Eminently characteristic was their form of " Thank you ! "—" *Revi-zelto !* "— God reigns, or God is here ! It was as if evil had failed to enter this land because of the very childheartedness of the race. The hissing creature had omitted to take up abode with them, since there was no charity to be done, or justice to be rendered, or punishment to be inflicted. Doubtless some beings would be very unhappy if they had not their little charities to administer, and the world would seem a dull place in which this pet luxury was taken from them— this peculiarly insidious form of the Devil's influence rooted out, and that homage we name nobly, "gratitude," claimed from the beggar for the penny given, denied them.

However, they were not unhappy in

Green Island, in spite of this serious
want: for, indeed, they were as those
living in a golden age, with little sorrow
and no evil to make weary their days.
Happiness seemed to be a rightful herit-
age of all; and it was even expounded by
some, who were given to serious thought,
that this state was as necessary to life
as air and food, or health, and that no
creature could thrive without a given
amount; but this, undoubtedly, was only
a subjective hypothesis, since they had
not yet learned to demonstrate the
truth of an idea by objective test.

*   *   *   *

In the darkest corner of space Satan
stood exulting in his sway over all lands.
His pale, beautiful countenance, illumined
by a white radiance emanating from his
person, bore the marks of everlasting pain
and eternal revolt.

Then the spirit Ferras, hideous and grinning, he who embodied the meanest attributes of his master, cried, " Nay, thou hast not yet conquered the Green Isle !" And the Master looked at him a while in silence, gazing at this strange, worm-white, mean creature who dared to stay the rejoicings of his pride.

" I might doubt my sovereignty, crawling viper, if, for loathsomeness, the sovereign claimed supremacy ! "

"I am thy creature,"answered the spirit.

" Thou lying one ! Thou darest not say 'e'en thy basest self'!"—and he paused ; then added : " What care I for such children as are of Green Island ? "

" Care ! Since thou art powerless 't would be of little avail ! But why remain powerless ? Hast thou ceased to wage still thy war, O Lucifer ? "

" For thee to devise a method !"

answered the Indomitable One. The creature at this command grew serious in thought, and the sickly grin went from his parched face, and his eyes fired with rapid thought as he pondered. At last he turned slowly, and with a look of exultant greed cried :

" THE POSSESSIVE PRONOUN ! "

Then a strange mocking laugh rose out of space and echoed down the filmy walls of the great atmosphere.

* * * *

Not many days had passed before a wondrous vessel, with sails gleaming in the gold of the sun, which pierced the stormy clouds and came down in a great shaft of light amidst the tossing crests of raging waves, neared the Island of Peace. And the people thereof watched her course, whilst the storm rose high in pitiless power, and giant clouds covered the face of the sun, and all the winds seemed in wild conflict, so that the ship was wrecked in the waste of the sea, and five men, naked and bruised, were dashed upon the mercy of her shores.

And the good people went down to the edge of the land, and led the exhausted survivors to shelter, and gave them raiments and food, showing them all such hospitality as lay in their power.

The dark new-comers seemed gracious men, and spoke the language of their hosts, with the addition of some odd words of which the Islanders had no wot of the meaning, sounding sinister and ugly to the unaccustomed ear, and at first no man had dared to ask explanation of them. But these visitors, who seemed to have come to stay, proved so amiable, and full of learning, that at last courage was found to broach the subjeet.

"Thou sayest 'mine': what meaneth the expression ?" said a youth.

The fatal word, once pronounced by their own people, was caught up and fled over the face of the Island quickly, from mouth to mouth, even as an overflowing river covereth the plains. And unconsciously those who uttered it tightened their grip of such things as they held, and greed came into the eyes of the lover as he gazed at his betrothed, and reluctance into those of the dispenser as he dealt out bread to the people.

The strangers laughed: they were seated, counting some gold coins saved from the wreck, in a cask, and they grasped more tightly the metal in their hands as they proceeded to explain, though the Islanders had shown no desire to possess what appeared to them but some kind of toy.

The explanation was long, and the many who gathered round to hear grew fascinated, though hardly understanding.

"You see," continued the eldest of the strangers, "it is wise that house and property should be your own, so that you can save for a time when food might be scarce, and ensure you and your wives and children from want!"

"Nay," answered the Islanders, "but what you say seems foolish, for should we not have to give part of our store to those who were without? Therefore it would no longer be our own."

"Why should you give to those who had not heeded to save? On the contrary, shut your doors, and bid them live as you have lived, abstaining, and without doubt they could do so, and learn the lesson of thrift!"

"Then, surely, things would even be as they are now?" laughed the crowd, so that the strangers waxed angry. "But," repeated the youth, "we are willing that ye call the houses ye live in yours—if ye will; we see no harm, only little use, good stranger!"

So things were left, and the Islanders went into house and jested over such ways, and the children, in sport, used the odd words till they grew accustomed to the sound. Thus the seed was sown down in their hearts—first in jest, then habit forgot, and found serious meaning, and wise use, in the words.

Gradually a strange change took place. The strangers, who had come to these shores ragged and hungry, kept to themselves all that they found for their use, and built higher walls round the houses they lived in. The people, who knew no reason why they should act in this way, began to follow in like manner. Then arose disputes as to what each had a right to claim, and they went to the foreigners to settle such disputes ; and the foreigners settled these things, but demanded portions of land or property in return for the trouble, and so well did they explain the justice of all this, that the people marvelled at such reasoning and knowledge, and were content.

For a time things went thus ill, seeming well enough; the Islanders grew less intimate with one another, and he who had found favour with the judge was shunned by the neighbour who had not.

Thus enmity grew up in their hearts, and even amongst the little children disputes arose, so that they followed in the steps of those parents who had ceased to respect them, those parents who quarrelled openly before them, and even commanded that they should pass their neighbour without salute. The old maxim, " Parents, respect the little children," was heard no more ; only, continually, " Children, respect your parents and superiors." But the children did not ; for how could they, young and unreasoning, when their parents respected not them ?

Thus evil grew in man's disposition ; evil, called wrongly by many "human nature," throve in the soil where good had been chased out, even as the weed takes root on the untended ground.

So pride and envy and greed had entered their homes, and those of the Green Island were happy no more.

And some, through advantage of better soil, grew rich and idle ; and others worked all day, but could not raise sufficient food for their families ; and they became despondent and careless, and envied and hated the successful.

And it happened, when in dire want, one man laughed aloud, saying: "But I have nothing now, not even to eat, and they deny me food. Why, I can but go and take some, as in the old time." And, knowing naught of wrong in so doing, since surely he had a right to live as well as they, he went forth and did this thing.

Then was the first man cast into prison,—cast into prison by those strangers from the seas whom he had befriended in their sore need. For they had grown rich from the spoil of the poor, and the people had elected them governors.

Therewith things grew ever worse. The sons of the strangers succeeded to their fathers, and the poor grew e'en poorer in working, and the rich richer in idleness. The use of money had crept in and the natural changed to the "competitive" or market value.

Then a famine fell on the land, and those who suffered knocked at the doors of the rich and asked for food, and they were denied; and they went in a crowd, indignant, at last to the Governors' house, and threatened to burn it there, if relief for their hungry children was not afforded; so that the Governors were obliged to notice them, and, with no little inward trepidation, but much outward show of equanimity, came, accompanied by armed servants, down from their palaces to the open in solemn procession, clad, not in their usual bright garments, but in sombre draperies, inoffensive to the ragged rabble : the jewelled raiments were within, hanging on pegs, to be donned at the feast when these tiresome affairs were over.

The gravity of their countenances and the solemn proceedings awed the crowd. Long orations were delivered, seeming full of sympathy for the distressed and just propositions for the alleviation of suffering. They alluded to the immense benefits of the splendid system which had brought education and the money-market to the Island, and to the great institutions of law and charity which rose up in grand edifices over the face of the whole country. Then they pro-ceeded—as the people, carried away by the innate delight of grandiloquence, cheered—to lay their proposition before them.

At first a groan went through the crowd, as it was understood that they were asked to dig for certain minerals under the

ground every day and all day ! And for
this service those who owned the land
would find support for them and their
families ! Rage leapt in their hearts—but
they were hungry !——

Thus the free men entered into ser-
vitude, and even the women ; and as the
new generation sprang up the remembrance of other times died. Under
the ground they toiled in darkness all the
days of their life ; and if, sometimes, the
old desire for pleasure and freedom over-
mastered them, and they went out for
some days and laughed and sang and
drank of the poison their masters made
for others' consumption—drank to drown
the remembrance of the long hours spent
below the fair, flowery earth—their idle
brothers quoted this as a sign of innate
evil, and breathed " blackguards " of those
who kept *them* in luxury and *their* wives

in silk, and who for generations worked without murmuring.

And Satan in one strange, wild moment of pity—or was it contempt?—cried: "Revolt! War! Kill your oppressors!" But Ferras answered: "Nay, Master; out of this would come good. With such thou hast nothing to do!" And the look of everlasting pain deepened on the Master's face, till eternal rage gleamed there again.

FABIUS THE BEAN-SOWER

FABIUS THE BEAN-SOWER

An Allegory

" And fear not them which kill the body,
but are not able to kill the soul."
MATTHEW x. 28.

THE green mountains undulated away
on all sides from where he stood, and the
blue canopy overhead seemed to end at
their farthermost line. The world, to the
boy, was a great verdant place of hill and
vale, with few trees and many flowers—
little violet stars on the heights, nestling
in between the very blades of grass ; and
yellow balls, and golden cups, and saffron
bells in the valleys, near to where silver
threads of hastening water wound about

the more level way, and tumbled in foaming laughter over stony impediments. He wore, girthed about his fair limbs, a skin of some wild creature ; his eyes reminded one of the gentians at his feet, and had something of their starry look ; the sunlight seemed to nestle in his hair and creep through his curling locks to line them with its gold ; his red, curved lips were parted as if in anticipated pain, and the gleaming teeth closed in seeming forbearance.

He stood, tall and slender, tapering from shoulders to ankle, that curved out again to feet which clung with naked tenacity to the yielding turf ; his fair form was silhouetted against the enshrining green, and the beauty everywhere appeared to culminate in the central figure of the lovely boy Fabius, the son of Ermas.

He dropped his arms, which had been stretched outward in a kind of despairing embrace of the verdant world, and sped away with lithesome movement to a grey hut lying in the lap of a small hollow on the hill before him. He stood irresolute at the door ; then, with a sigh, lifted the latch and entered into the dark of a low-roofed room, with but one small window set, like a jewel, in the dusky walls of the hut : the outward aspect of emerald gleamed within.

" Thou art quite sure," he said, addressing two figures busily counting seeds, " thou art quite sure thou wouldst have me go to the Black Town to work with Master Silas ? Will it not suffice that I mind the white lambs on the hill, that I dig the ground and sow the seeds of corn, and trim the climbing vine ? Will not this, my service, from when the sun riseth over yonder points till it setteth again behind the cottage, suffice thee ? "

" Nay, we are decided : we would have thee go and work for gold," Ermas answered :

" Hast thou not enough gold in the broad beams of sunlight which turn the green oats yellow for our food, and warm the heart of the vine, that its fruit may be plentiful for our consumption ? "

" Enough, thou art a dreamer."

" Nay, I am but a bean-sower."

" We would have thee bring gold—gold from the earth's bowels.   Dost hear ? "

" Nay, my father and mother, and will it not harden our hearts ? "

As he thus spake a laugh broke from the aged people: the old man rose, seeming a giant near the slender boy, and stretched out a sinewy arm to catch at his son.

" When thy heart," he said, in scoffing accents, " is hard with too much gold, then bring it hither, and we will rid thee of it, though we tear thy girlish flesh to get at it."

Their laugh echoed about the boy's ears, and he shrank from the hand that threatened him even in pleasantry.

"Then good-bye," he said, and moved nearer his mother.

"Good-bye," quoth she, in a hurry, and continued to count her seeds.

Therewith he turned and went away.

The long, fiery arms of the setting sun seemed to clasp the hill-tops in an angry grasp as Fabius, with tears in his blue eyes, sped down the precipitous path to the dark town, far distant in the plain. Some young lambs raised their heads, then hurried together to a point, and bleated as their shepherd passed below : a stray goat rubbed its horny head against his knees, then followed part of the way down the steep.

Still the lad sped on . . . " But *she* is my mother and *he* is my father," he murmured ever and anon, and the stones sprang from under his feet and led the way before in a dizzy rush.

Spreading far beneath was the great grey plain lying in the shadow of the mountain : a dark river intersected it like a curving snake with wet gleaming body.

On the banks stood the Black City.

At nightfall he entered the gates. The glare of lights shimmered here and there, revealing the blackest of the Black City's blackness, and noise, everywhere, stunned the youth with its boisterous greeting. Sudden knots of people revelled before him and then dispersed, to disappear like phantoms through shadowy arches or un-perceived ways, whilst new comers loitered into notice, their unhallowed voices jarring suddenly on the ear. None paid heed to the boy from the hills as he stole, like a frightened creature, to the heart of the city and lay himself down under a great wall in a deserted square. He stretched his full length and closed his eyelids, now heavy with desire of sleep, when he was disturbed by a fitful light which flashed on the buildings about and startled him to sudden wakefulness. He crouched nearer the stone-work as a medley of riotous youths, bearing torches, crossed the square.

"To the Enchanted Princess!" cried one, and raised a cup of wine to his lips; the toast resounded through the crowd with ribald glee. "To her sad eyes!" said a pale boy, and a shout of laughter rose and re-echoed as they passed by, grey silence spreading wide in their wake. "To her white arms!" was borne back on the wave of sound.

Fabius flushed carnation pink, and tossed his head to breathe a fresher air ; then he smiled and looked long upwards, for there were stars here too, and the great glorious heavens were over the Black City even as over the hills.

Then his golden head fell in sleep, and he dreamed that the Enchanted Princess looked at him down from the glimmering stars.

*　　　*　　　*　　　*

"Who is the Enchanted Princess?" demanded Fabius on the third day of his work at the iron forge.

"Hush!" said his companion, and the boy thought the laugh he gave was forced.

Later he questioned again some apprentices : "Tell me of the Enchanted Princess?"

"Faith, if thou keepest so serious a face thou wilt not work long here !" whispered one. "Our master doth not like the matter spoken of, unless in jest!"

"What of the Enchanted Princess?" persisted Fabius to another.

"I know naught of such things," he answered. "They say she is charmed by an evil spirit; but it's all nonsense, I dare swear!"

"Her lips are red as wine and she loveth well," quoth another, and he laughed so that Fabius blushed.

Some time after he had spent many days and nights in the city, he sat, one midday, eating bread with a knot of fellow-workers, when the master came by and accused one of speaking too seriously of the Enchanted Princess.

"Good only with our drink!" said he.

"Nay, we were but laughing," they answered.

"Thou may'st take thy fill of laughter

at the maid, 'tis good for such young as thou—for thy pleasure—but ye all know the penalty of serious converse concerning the enchanted minx, the very existence of whom, in truth, is but a myth.   I will have no one here, however well he work, who talketh in seriousness of such folly."

"But if she be troubled," said Fabius, "may we not help her?   If she be chained, as some have told, could we not break the irons with our hammers?   Surely laughter will never free her!"

"Cease, thou stripling!   Who hath filled thy head with such stories?"—and he strode away in anger.   And those about Fabius smote him for a fool who had betrayed them.

But time went its quick way, and the boy still pondered on the Princess, and when he heard their ribald words of her he would turn away, sick at heart, albeit he could not help at times questioning them concerning her; so that at last they began to point at him, and jeer, and shun his society. Then the days seemed long indeed and cheerless, and the work grew heavy to the unused hands, and the light went from the gentian eyes, and the mouth was like a red stain on the pale face, and he longed for the blue hills wearily.

So it happened one morning that the boy, deep in thought, exclaimed aloud, not seeing the master near at hand: " But where doth she dwell, the Enchanted Princess?" Wherefore they turned him out into the noisy street by the great river.

Fabius stood bewildered. He gazed down into the black, moving volume of slow, unreflecting waters; then the thought of a mountain rivulet babbled in his fancy, and, hardly realising what had happened,

33 C

only conscious of his freedom, the boy leapt the bridge, and fled down the narrow streets and across the sunless square as one pursued.

He escaped out of the gates and traversed the great plain with eager haste, so that when he turned at last to look back the Black City lay far below at his feet.

With a cry of exultant joy he threw himself down in the long grass, and kissed the green blades which pressed on his cheeks, and, at the warm touch of the sun-wooed earth, dug his nails into the soft ground with passionate reiteration.

He tossed away the superfluous draperies the Black City had forced him to wear, and kicked, in free delight, his boyish limbs, which gleamed in the waving grass and scintillating sunlight. Blue butterflies fell flapping on his body, and tiny black ones sailed round his golden head, whilst a great bee hummed about, and the grass-hoppers trilled—a thousand voices every-where—and he laughed to keep them company, moving gently with his hand a stray leaf, that a fat beetle might continue its solemn march; then his eyelids drooped from fatigue of so hasty a journey, and, with a smile still lurking near his lips, he fell asleep.

When Fabius awoke the world around was drowsing in the grey shadows of the coming even, and as he sprang to his feet the last rim of the day's beacon had shot beneath the horizon, and a quick breeze rose over the hills and bowed the tips of the long grass in a silver wave of motion. He thrilled with the sense of it; then started forward up the steep path, stretching an arm to grasp a bramble or projecting stone thereby to help his spring; for he had lost much strength in those days spent in the plain, so that he grew quite wearied as he went.

But on the summit new vigour leapt within his veins, and, full riotous with laughter, he beat an entry on the cottage door.

"Who's there?" came from within.

"'Tis I, thy son Fabius!" he shouted : then he bent his head and caught the sound of a shuffling gait. The door slowly opened, and the giant figure of Ermas loomed from out the uncertain light of the cottage; he peered at his son with unsteady eye, and Fabius guessed at wine in the cup he held.

"Thou! And thy gold? Hast brought gold with thee?"

The boy's hands drooped to his side and his lips trembled as he stammered :

"Nay, but I have no gold. They sent me away, and I did forget my wage, for I was

36

overjoyed to come back to thee—I thought of naught but home."

"Thou crazy creature! And wherefore did Master Silas send thee forth?"

"He is more cunning than crazy," cried Martha, his mother, in anger; she was still counting her seeds at the table. "For without doubt he hath spent this money in the city and doth fool us with excuses: see how pale he wears!"

"'Twas for the Enchanted Princess," said Fabius, and his eyes lit up with a strange and lovely light.

"Thou darest to mock us, thou white imp!" roared Ermas, and therewith he laid hands on the boy and beat him till he fell senseless—the blood in coloured blemishes streamed on the white of his skin and bespattered the gold of his hair. Then rudely they took him and laid him on his bed, up the wooden stairs without, in a

low-roofed chamber, and locked the door
upon him.

* * * *

A stream of sudden light filled the little
room, and Hope, winged with feathers of
iridescent green, stood upon the threshold,
and Fabius awoke, crying: "Nay, but I
will to the Black City, and demand the
wages my due; only stay thy hand from
beating me, for it hurteth sorely!"

Then a soft voice, like the murmuring
of the wind, called "Fabius!" and a cool
breath, as if caused by the beating of
wings on the air, swept over his couch, and
he started up in fear: "Who calleth?"
and Hope answered back:

"Wouldst thou free the Enchanted
Princess?" and the starry eyes of Fabius
looked up in wonder.

"What availeth my aid if thou hast
failed, winged spirit?"

"I am thou," answered the angel, and the boy stretched out his hands and cried :

"Then teach me how I may be thee!" And the wings of Hope spread wide as she stooped and kissed his mouth.

The walls fell in darkness about them and quick winds hurried by.

"Look up, Fabius!"

And Fabius raised his eyes and saw that they stood in a great hall, and he clutched the hand of Hope as the mist before them dissolved.

High above she was seated, the Enchanted One ; on a black marble throne she sat, her hair like broad ribbons of saffron gold entwining its dusky surface.

Her white arms stretched out to guide the spinning-wheel, and in her eyes there dwelt a whole world of pathos, the weariness of anticipated joy never come.

She spun, and as she spun there came a pattern of a heart upon her cloth, and when in clear outline it appeared, a drop of blood fell from her own heart and dyed it crimson red, and she sighed as butterfly wings finished the design ; and she went on to weave another heart, dyeing it again with her own blood ; but still the wings of butterflies grew, and another sigh echoed through the still atmosphere.

"Why doth she spin thus?" quoth Fabius, "and why doth she sigh so?"

" She is in this way enchanted," Hope answered, " until a heart shall appear on her cloth broken in two, and on which there shall be no wings—only then will the spell be broken ; but if within a given time such cometh not she will die from the loss of her heart's blood."

"Nay," said Fabius, "she shall not die!"

And his voice resounded through the wide
hall, and the Princess turned her head,
and for one moment her sad eyes rested
on his ; then a great noise thundered
about him, and glinting metals flashed
on his sight, and he found himself in
a vast work-place, hammering on iron :
the din of grinding wheels and beating
metals echoed and re-echoed against the
walls, and huge and hideous machines
hissed out on the air from the confines of
their gnashing teeth.

Several youths were at work, and their
faces were young and beautiful, their
tunics of soft draperies embroidered at
the hem. Near to where they stood was
a great gaping hole, from which emerged
the groans of crunching rollers : for a
moment Fabius peered in, to shrink back
in horror from the swaying mass of
whirring steel and swollen, jointed

machinery, vibrating with a seemingly impotent greed; yet fear had no part in his horror.

"Who cometh?" he asked of his companion, later, as a tall figure entered, clad in plain white, with neither fold nor seam, and a hood about his head.

"'Tis Master Ambition!" answered a youth, and as the figure passed silently along, looking at none, each seemed to work the better; but Fabius caught the face beneath the cowl, and there looked at him but the hollow cavities of a skull's head, and Fabius trembled and worked but ill. Then angry voices made him turn, and there a creature, with vicious eyes and stunted figure, robed in a gown of richest gold, threatened a youth, who, pale before him, stammered weak-hearted protests.

"Who is he?" pressed Fabius.

"Master Gold, our master; the youth no doubt hath dreamed of the Princess, which it is forbidden here to do. He will be thrown into the machinery of the world."

"Where is the machinery of the world?"

"In the great chasm at our feet!"

But as the apprentice was about to fall he leapt, and a door opened suddenly to save him; then Fabius again saw the Enchanted One, the black of her throne, the gold of her hair, the white of her arms, and the spell of her eyes; and again the wings came upon her cloth, again her blood dyed the heart red, again she sighed—and the vision passed.

"Did he love the Princess?" he asked.

"Aye."

And Fabius was silent.

Three days he worked, and one by one

43

the lovers fled in fear from the vengeance of their master, and every time the blue-eyed one looked sadly from her throne, and her blood dyed yet another winged heart. Each day Ambition silently walked through—each day Gold warned, then threatened—each day there was one worker the less—each day a winged heart the more!

"And thou?" quoth the master in sudden fury, as Fabius stood dreaming on the fourth day, "have I not warned thee ofttimes?"

"I care not for thy warning!" the intrepid one answered, so that the stunted master doubled up with very rage, and put an ugly hand round the lovely body of the youthful worker, who struggled not, though he paled as when death comes.

And in the black chasm of grinding

steel Fabius the bean-sower was crushed —Fabius the gentian-eyed.

Ah! the pain, the pain! Would it never cease? Surely not eternal pain? Ah! pity, pity!

Then all had ending, and he woke with his head in the lap of the Princess, her face quite near to his, and the sorrow gone from her eyes.

*　　*　　*　　*

Ermas, in the cold light of early dawn, crept up the wooden stair, and opened the creaking door. He had resolved to send his son back to the Black City even now; but he stopped on the threshold in sudden fear, and called Martha his wife. Guiltily they crawled to the bed, hand in hand, then white and shrivelled they looked at one another, for Fabius was dead; and about his body was wrapped a wondrous cloth with a little broken heart woven thereon.

MERIEL

MERIEL

" *And all our righteousnesses are as filthy rags.*"

Isaiah lxiv. 6.

With Wisdom grey by her side, Meriel rested at last on the Earth's yielding surface, and with bated breath peered at the World—the wondrous world of gleaming water tossing and laughing at her feet and of green soft plains—in repeated waves immutable and still—retreating far, to rise at last in jagged points high into the unreflecting glimmer of the skies, tremulous, at this early hour, with the first touch of the rising sun. She sat with a certain laughing fear in her

49   D

gleaming, inquisitive eyes, and pressed with chary touch the bladed turf about her ; then tried to catch with lifted fingers the breath of wind which tossed her long hair in a floating red aureole wide.

"I would for ever stay here," she murmured ; " the World is fairer than all the stars in starry space." And the Spirit of Wisdom answered :

" Stay, Meriel, until such beauty fill thy heart with wearied pain."

" Thou art ever serious, good Wisdom," she returned. " Thou hast steered me here through seeming endless darkness, through angry storms of wrestling elements which encircle only this strange globe, lovelier than all her sisters—and now thou wouldst have me go ! Nay, I fain would stay ; so, good-bye."

She rose, with arms uplifted, in playfulness to drive her unwanted companion hence, then turned and went her way. She danced on the green sward, her purple draperies as wings outspread ; then chased the breeze in gleeful race.

She tried to touch the gold of the sun's first rays, and crouched low down at the sight of a tree, thinking the outspread branches would take her, unwilling, in their grasp ; but when she crawled at last under the leafy umbrage, she laughed again at the gleaming lights without, which tried to gain an entry between the leaves.

Thus Meriel wandered about the sweet earth—through her woods and by her rivulets, among her flowers or with her falling waves.

And as she walked on a rocky way, near the sea, yet shadowed by trees which edged a grassy place stretching to cornfields bounded again by wood, she rested for some moments, when a youth, beautiful as the morning and sad even as the night, came to where she was and looked into her eyes.

"Who art thou?" she questioned, dreaming naught of audacity. And he smiled so that she knew he was sad, so sad was his smile.

"Who art *thou*, who hast a look of other worlds in thine eyes, and who knowest not of one whom they once called Love, but since have named Sin?"

Full of wonder, she said: "Why do they call thee Sin?"

The youth turned and looked at the far sea, a blue ribbon seeming to divide the white of the heavens from the green of the land:

"I know not—perhaps because they mistake me for my twin-brother, who is mad, and to whom they have given the name of Vice."

" Where is he ? "

" He roameth about, wild, unclad and hungry, in the woods. Should he emerge in daytime they would stone him and in chains bear him publicly to prison."

" And at night ? "

" They steal out, masked, and carry food to him : so that he who would die liveth by their hands."

" Canst thou do naught ? "

" Nay, for when I do pursue him he flieth, and where *I* am there *he* never is."

Something of sadness crept over the face of Meriel, and she stretched out a hand, saying : " I am sorry for thee ! Wilt thou come and pick flowers with Meriel ? "

" Art thou not afraid, Meriel, of the World ? "

" The World ? No ; why should I be afraid ? It seems all kindness, this lovely world, with flowers growing even at our feet! I had dreamed of flowers, but never of such fragrant blossoms as these! And then the wide, leaved trees to shade one weary of too much sun—and such a silver stream to babble music in our ears! —and the great sea, which threatens in playfulness to depart, and, creeping away, riotously comes laughing back! Why wouldst thou have me afraid?"

"But I have an evil name!"

"Then we will change thy name." She smiled, but the smile died before it was full grown by reason of the strange appearance of a woman nearing them, who wore no garments, albeit her hands were swathed in coverings.

"Who cometh this way? Look how she treadeth down the corn!"

"'Tis Virtue, so-called," said the youth. "She weareth gloves, and her hair is parted down the middle!"

" Thou likest her not ? "

" She speaketh unwonted truths about her friends, and lieth about herself ! "

"Wherefore lieth she ? "

" She doth but what she is !"

"Thou speakest as Sin would—denying good ! "

" Nay, I deny not goodness—it dwelleth with us still," he answered, and was silent.

" Where ? " she pleaded in gentle atonement.

" In the heart of a peasant, and in the soul of a poet."

"Are there many poets and peasants?"

"Yea, more than all others."

" Then Goodness reigneth on this fair Earth, which in all her beauty challengeth that we love her not, knowing we are wholly hers—surely we *will* love her, since Goodness reigneth ? "

55

"Nay, Meriel, the 'others' rule. Peasants and poets go in rags, whilst the world liveth on the poor man's produce, and when the hungry ask for food, Dame Virtue, from her gilded throne in the public square, giveth a penny and buyeth the name of Charity."

"Thou talkest of naught but ugly things, sir youth, and I would fain not have met thee!" and Meriel turned her look from him, even in anger.

"I am grieved to grieve thee, gentle one. A herald, once, of joy, I have been to thee but a messenger of pain . . . . yet it is for sorrow for that bleeding heart—the human heart of this thy lovely World, which knoweth only of sad love—I beg thy pity. In labour and poverty joyous love hath starved. In luxury and sin joyous love hath died."

Then the fair youth, beautiful as the

morning and sad even as the night, turned
and went away.

Meriel watched him go, and, when she
could see him no more, she tossed her hair
and caught some meshes between her
gleaming teeth, then sang a little song to
cheat herself from sadness.

She wandered further along the path, her
purple draperies clinging now V-wise down
to her little feet, her red-crowned head of
wondrous hair drooped ; and though the
starry flowers, the yellow-hearted daisies,
peered up at her from their dark myrtle-
green beds, they only seemed to Meriel
like tears fallen from Sin's sad eyes.

And she came to where some men were
labouring in a field. They bent low over
the ground and toiled sadly, unconscious
of the floods of sunshine around them.
They were as dark and unseemly patches
on the fair landscape to Meriel, for the

grim, weather-beaten faces lacked the beauty of the sad youth she had just quitted, and Necessity seemed to have chased even sorrow from their countenances to engrave her own hard image on them.

Not far off lounged some youths, in soft clothes, watching.

"Ye seem to be working hard, good friends," she said: "there are some idle lads quite near who look tired from very weariness of doing nothing—will they not help ye?"

And the rough men all laughed, and continued their labour, and Meriel knew not why they laughed, and said again in question: "They have an holiday?"

"Yea," answered one, "every day of the year and every year of their lives!"

"But how get they food, if they help not to procure their substance? Surely they will find but a scanty meal to-night?"

Again the men laughed, and their laugh echoed harshly, and Meriel grew frightened, for such a laugh is, indeed, the ugliest of all human sounds—it speaks of tragedy without dignity, rage without use, and hatred combined with the impotence of despair and the necessity of *virtueless* resignation. And she moved away; but as she went they said :

"'Tis we who will have poor fare !"

And she thought they were mocking her, so that she hastened from their company till she was alone again near the shore. Lifting her head with a sigh, she looked before her, where, leaning against a tree, a grey-haired man stood, with raised, contemplative head.

She stood quite still to look at him, and a thought of the Spirit of Wisdom came to her, yet there was more in his face ; it was not Pity, or Sorrow, or Love, or Hope, or Power, or Strength, or Knowledge, or

Truth, or Wit; neither of the Judge or the
Advocates, the Teacher or the Doer, the
Hero or the Labourer; yet something of
all these attributes, of all these powers, lived
in the keen, sensitive visage whose impenetrable eyes gave no quarter to weak-
ness. Meriel felt desire to bend a knee;
then she looked to where he gazed, and
there, from the wood, emerged two pro-
cessions, and wound down the path to the
sea. They were women all, and young;
the half were clad in white soft garments;
they had fair sweet faces and soft tresses
of hair; they smiled as they went, and
seemed to know of naught but happiness.
Near to them walked those others, young,
yet seeming born old, in tattered gowns or
gaudy raiments, who laughed likewise, but
loudly and harshly: the unhallowed sound
echoed on the air; their girlish faces were
bedaubed with carmine, and now and then

they threw a mocking jest at a near sister in spotless attire, who recoiled back with horror to the shelter of her friends. Nefarious, wanton words grappled for supremacy, and befouled the air with poisonous breath as they emerged from even childish lips.

Then Meriel stood, tall in anger, and cried : "Who are those vile creatures who walk so near to women? Who are they who cheat us into thinking they may be women too? What strange and devilish reflection of our own selves lurks within their eyes? Who are they who dare to ape womanhood?"

The old man answered in measured words :

" They are thus vile that their sisters may be virtuous—thus ill-clad that those others should wear white—impure that they by their side may be pure."

"Know good women this thing?" breathed Meriel.

"No, they think their own gift heaven-given and their sisters' by their own sin begotten. And if by chance one in gentle kindness stretcheth a hand to help one fallen thus, Virtue and Maternity whisper in her ear, '*They must be!*' And should she answer the lie with question: 'If the demand be no wrong, wherefore should the supply be sin?' Virtue shuddereth and putteth on her gloves: but Truth shrieks out with finger pointed at these pure, loveless maids who sell not for bread, but for luxury:

"The Reserve!"

*   *   *   *

Meriel crouched on the ground, her face quite near the blades of grass, which caught the tears as they sped down her cheeks. Then she rose and said : " Is there no help ? "

And the old man answered with seeming fire in his eyes :

" No, not till good women go down on bended knees and ask forgiveness of these poor wanton ones, saying : ' We have wronged ye, even we ! ' "

" And shall it happen ? "

He turned his head and looked at the sea crimsoned by the setting of the great disc, and murmured :

" When Pity, chased by Gold to some far sphere, returns, or is born again, and Love bringeth her back to Earth—only then !" Therewith he rose and with shuffling gait passed into the wood ; and Meriel cried softly: "Pity shall come back!"

Then she turned and went to the very edge of the sea, and the red light reddened all her garments, and Love came to where

63

she was, and, kneeling down, looked into her eyes, and, seeing tears there, wiped them with his hand away :

"Meriel I have waited long for thee!"

And she put her palm upon his palm and said :

"We will go and look for Pity, Love, thou and I—through starry space we will seek for Pity, thou and I!"

*   *   *   *

Then Love and Meriel left the World of flowers and sin. And the last ray of ruddy light dyed the woods a deep red, even like the colour of blood, and there echoed over the land the wanton laugh of the mad twin-brother they called Vice.

PHILE

E

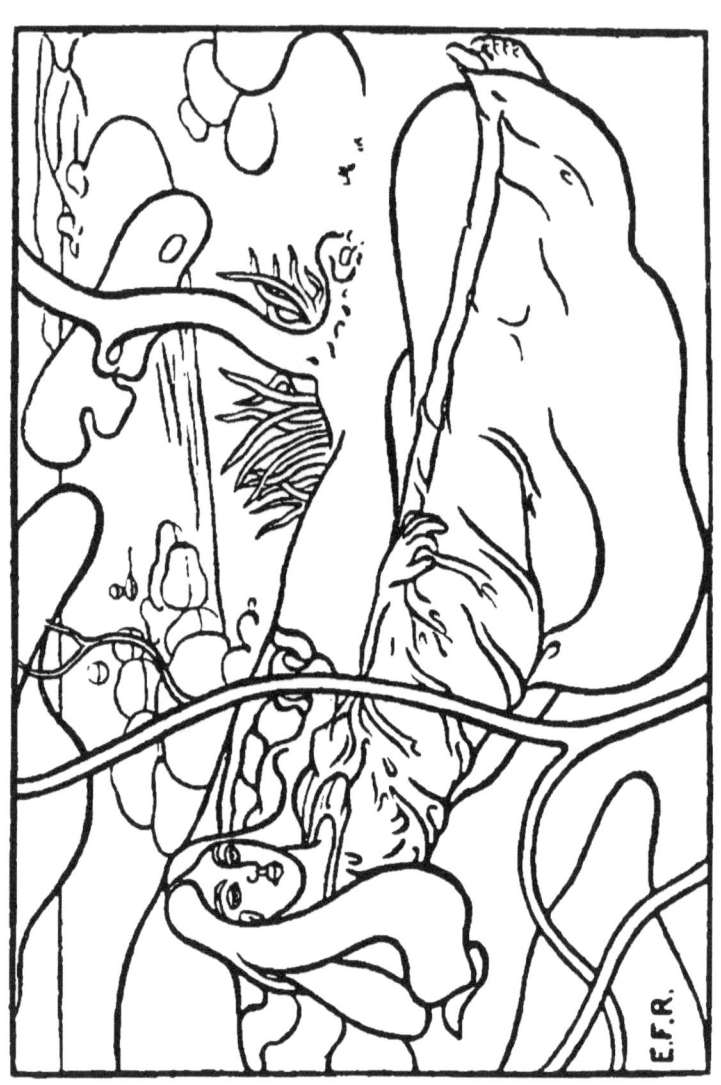

PHILE

THE enemy kings were friends at last, and the son of the one was thereupon betrothed to the fair daughter of the other, and nothing of the young people's inclination was asked, for each was beautiful and young and rich, and endowed with every attribute that most befits the child of a king.

When the day of the marriage came, all the splendour was displayed customary at a festivity of such royal import. The dark cedar-trees were decked with bright-coloured shields emblazoned with two kings' arms, and garlands hung upon them of wondrous flowers.

The little children danced for joy and laughed, and tossed the roses at one another, whilst the youths sported in the open, and the old men pressed the juice from the grapes into silvern goblets for the women to drink thereof.

Great banners waved in the air, scented from the garlands of flowers, and the voices of singing boys were borne upon the breeze.

The poor forgot their poverty in such revelry, and the hungry were fed. The very sunshine seemed to take part in the festivity, and dazzled all in its golden fury, cheating brightness from the dullest stones, and creeping through fretted leaves to spread a yellow carpet at their feet.

Light and laughter dwelt everywhere

but in the sad eyes of the Princess and the cold countenance of him she had wedded, as they passed among the shouting people. The kings, their fathers, rode before, united at last in a haughty friendship through the betrothal of their children. Greed for wealth had separated these iron warriors, and greed for more had united them : but the smile on their faces was set, and, indeed, the poor, ragged man had more joy in his countenance who said : " Faith ! I have naught to be happy for, but I will be gay since the rich appear to be much rejoicing." Yet withal the bride seemed as one in sorrow : her head drooped as a wilted flower, and her cheeks were whiter than the lilies in her crown. For in her heart there dwelt the remembrance of a knight still most dear to her, and she knew not how to forget him.

And the bridegroom looked wearily

69

over the crowd and omitted to seek the smile of his bride.

And it was murmured among his friends that a maid far away was weeping for him.

The procession swept by, and the people wotted naught of such sorrow; but only gazed in wonder at the rich garments of fine spun gold the royal heirs wore, and laughed because it was good to laugh. How could they dream a *Prince* was sad?

Then a wild hurrah echoed from side to side, and gleaming swords flashed in the air, and a blast of trumpets heralded the entrance of the Prince and Princess to their home—a home resplendent with all the beauty of art's most precious labour: statues wrought in gold and silver; pale ivory faced with fiery orbs of jewels; hangings of richest purple with star-flowers interwoven near the edge—

red-hearted, for the love they symbolised
—such a dwelling-place as must render
happy those who lived therein.

Yet he led her through the painted
halls with no look of happiness. The
sound of the tumult without grew fainter
on their ears as they went, till it quite
ceased, and they found themselves alone
in a great chamber.

They stood before the open window
in silence, for they had nothing to say
to one another. A breath of warm, un-
knowing wind tossed the gauzy draperies
on her breast; but she laid a cold hand
to still them, and the wind shivered and
went its way.

He looked to the west, where the sun
was sinking and the hill-tops were edged
with a streak of red light, and he thought
of that other maid. And she raised her
sad eyes to the east, pale in the glimmer

of the rising moon, and prayed not to think unloyally.

He caught her pained look, yet guessed not the reason thereof, and was sorry, seeing she was helpless. So he put forth his hand and gathered a fresh rose which clung to the casement without, and offered it to her; but the petals fell one by one to their feet, and the kind speech died on his lips even as a sigh on the air.

Spring fled to summer and autumn to winter, and the young Prince passed the time in hunting, and the Princess dwelt in the topmost tower with her face turned to the east, and fashioned strange devices in tapestry. And though there was much noise of revelry in the palace and outward show of festivity, though all discussed the ball of yesterday and the great hunt of the morrow in apparent good humour, a gloom seemed to settle in the very midst of their wildest gaieties, and the youths of the Court became cynical and overdressed; and, because they sought only pleasure, pleasure ceased to please, and life became burdensome to them; and some were known who stole away, disguised, to find happiness where this strange soul-sickness of the loveless Court had not penetrated. And then it came that the Princess bore a son, and she died in giving it life, and as she died her last thought was for the knight in the east: and the gloom deepened over the palace when it was known that because there had been no love at his begetting the child was born without a heart.

*   *   *   *

As was his custom, the Prince was far from home, wearily whipping his steed to gain still a new road, that he might dream through its strangeness that he were not the Prince of Telmaris, and that his heart did not long to go west to the maid far away. Then witchery turned his bridle, and the great black horse bore him swiftly from the east, since Conscience had outwitted herself and, pale in dilemma, said "Go"; but a cold hand smote him in the face, and the dark creature reared high, then dashed on a wild career, for the Prince of two kingdoms was dead.

*　　*　　*　　*

The little babe waxed strong and fair, and as he grew to childhood, then to youth and manhood, many marvelled at his strange intelligence and wondrous beauty; but none spoke of his love or charity, or his smiles; for the young Prince had no heart, and naught pleased him, and he cared for naught.

Only, just before eventide, he was wont

to stray on the seashore, and, resting on the rocks, watch, ever expressionless, the vast stretch of level water for many hours together, as if that hope he lacked might come from over the limitless horizon, and give him that which the poorest creature possessed.

Now there dwelt, near to where the surf whitened the edge of the land, a young girl called Phile, and she lived alone in a small stone house and mended the net of fishermen.

She heard of the Prince who was born without a heart, who knew nothing of sorrow, neither òf joy, who loved not nor hated, who was wise in all things and beautiful as the Sun-God, and she watched him come every evening and go, and there grew up in her heart a great love and pity for him, so that she would creep out among the rocks and sit near to where he was, half hidden, at his feet. Therefore it happened that he noticed her, and he spoke to her, and discoursed of many things —concerning the sea and the fish therein, and the heavens and the stars thereof ; and she hearkened with wide open eyes and breathed in his words in extasy. But when he had finished he went his way ; and she returned to her lonely little home with the mingled sense of joy and sorrow in her heart.

Next day at sunset he came, and as before he spoke to her, so that she was full of gladness whilst he was there, and when he was gone she was sad.

Many days passed in this way : all the happiness of the little fisherman's daughter was comprised in these moments at sunset, and afterwards in the anticipation of the morrow or the remembrance of the yesterday. As she mended her nets, catching up the broken threads and uniting them again, or weaving in a new cord, she thought of all the things he had told her, and laughed to herself from very pleasure in pondering on his words.

Sometimes the thought of the little bright fish, with their pearly sides, deterred her lithesome fingers : for she found pain in the consideration of how this brown, rough net was to hold them prisoners, and take them from their great sea to suffocate in the heavy air ; and she wished she might leave just a little hole that they could escape through ; and therewith she would desist from her work and go out and sit on the rocks far out to sea, and tell the little fish how she loved the Prince, and how sad he was, and how it were better to be as they, and even be caught at last and die, than to live without a heart.

And it happened that for several days he did not come, and the little maid grew very sad, and when at last he approached he made no move to speak to her, and she, forsaken, crept out to her rock and sang to the little fish.

The next time she saw him she noticed a wearied look on his face, as one over-burdened with indifference, and this look grew with the passing of the days, and Phile's pain, with pity for him, deepened almost to despair. One night she wandered out on the sands at that hour when the vaulted heavens are alight with shining stars, and she gazed up into their faces.

Would they not tell her how to serve the Prince ?

And a quick wind whistled past her ears, and she listened to the tumbling of the wild waves and the swoop of the

great birds' wings, and she cried aloud :
" World ! O World ! how can I give the
Prince a heart ? "

Then a voice from the darkness called
to her :

" Phile, Phile, if thou lovest well, take
thou a silver goblet to the fountain of
Eros and carry water therefrom, which
thou shalt bring to thy Prince to drink."
And the voice died on the breath of the
wind ; and Phile flew to her little cottage,
full of fear.

In the morning the sun crept through
her window and broke the spell of sleep
about her. And a soft voice murmured
in her ears : " Phile, Phile, if thou lovest
well " ; and she was no longer afeared,
and prepared such things as she should
need for the journey to the Fountain of
Eros. But when she was ready, then it
came to her that she had no silver goblet,

neither any money wherewith to buy one, and she sat down, sick at heart, and pondered long.

Now, with the maids of Telmaris it was a custom that every one should inherit from her mother a wedding-robe embroidered in silver and ofttimes jewels, and that she, in her turn, should bequeath it to her daughter, so that for many generations these vestments were handed from parent to child.

Phile was very poor, and her only possession was a like robe ; she cherished it with pride, and loved it, for it was all she had in the world, and there were silver daisies worked round the hem.

She thought now of it and knew she must sell it at the market-place. Forthwith she rose, and took it gently, and hurried out, not daring to glance at its shining folds, lest she should repent her.

And the girls at the market-place mocked and whispered unkind words ; for no maid sold her wedding-gown—at Telmaris 'twas deemed dishonour—and they turned away from her, and she felt the hot tears scalding her eyes as they whispered one to another: "Know you that Phile sells her wedding-robe ? Is she not shameless !" But Phile cried within her : "Nay, I do but sell it for love !"

And a merchant of the East noted her confusion, and the bright garment in her arms, and did take advantage thereof, and proffered but half the value for the raiment, saying : "One who sells her marriage-gown shall not make terms;" and he did leer at her, and Phile was afraid, so that she grasped the silver coins and fled as the girls and youths laughed and jeered at her.

She came to a seller of silver things

and she purchased a goblet, and inquired of him who sold it her the way to the Fountain of Eros; and he answered in haste that he knew not. Then a white dove rose up from the ground and flew south, and Phile understood she must go that way; so she tied the goblet to her girdle and went forth alone.

The road was rough, and sharp flints cut her naked feet, and there were no trees to shelter her from the sun, or flowers by the way to gladden her heart; but she sang a little song as she went, that she might not heed how sharp the stones were, or how dreary the aspect. A whole long day passed and the grey shadows of even spread round her, and still she sped over the ground, till dark night stayed her tired feet, and hunger denied her strength; then she rested on a rock by the way and ate of the bread she brought with her. All the next

day she walked, and the third day, and
likewise on the fourth, though she had no
more food ; and she came to the Fountain
of Eros, in a green place with tall trees
about it, and the bright water falling into
a sleek pool beneath where the grass-bank
hemmed it in. Phile raised her cup to
catch the water, and looked up into the
face of the young god, and for that moment
she was not weary ; then she turned and
went back as she had come, only she sang
not.

The road stretched a grey line before
the wayfarer far across the plain, and
there were low rocks on either side like
faceless creatures keeping guard, and the
sun was high and beat a white heat
down from the colourless heavens. The
path seemed even more rough, for her
feet were sore and cut, and her garment
torn about her ankles so that as she

stepped it was with difficulty she held the cup in such a manner that the water might not spill. Night came on when she had traversed but a little way, and, because she was faint and hungry, sleep fled from her, and she felt afraid in the great plain alone, as darkness encompassed all things, and silence seemed to echo back on her ears. Quite still she sat, still as the night about her, till morning came from very pity and covered the road with a glory of red.

For three more days Phile wandered alone; she had naught to eat or to drink and she slept not, and each night her fear grew greater.

At last the blue sea spread before her, and the salt breeze fanned her cheeks, and she sighed a little sigh of joy, "O my Prince! my Prince! I am coming! But at each step she faltered, and the breath would not come to her parched lips, and the hands which grasped the goblet were benumbed, and she knew not how she held it.

The sun was sinking over the sea in a blaze of royal colour, and shafts of golden light stretched from the red disc to the nethermost points of the heavens; and the Prince sat on the rocks and gazed before him, and knew not that Phile was near.

She stood quite still, and despair looked out of her eyes.

Then a young girl, passed by, with fair hair wafted by the wind and crowned with a wreath of flowers, and she sang as she came. Her eyes were blue like the heavens in daytime, and her lips red as wine, and white like the morning was the robe she wore. And Phile cried to her: "Nay, stop, pretty creature, and take for me this goblet of water to the Prince yonder, and make him drink thereof."

And the young girl laughed, and wonderingly took it in her hand, and danced on her way to the Prince.

He rose as she came, and drank of the water she offered, then he gave her back the silver cup and his hand did meet hers in the returning of it, and through a long full gaze their eyes in one another's lived. She smiled as he kissed her face, as the waves kissed the rocks at her feet, and hand in hand they wandered down on the shore through the red of the lover's sun, and they came to the body of Phile stretched across their path—and she was dead!

And it was because they loved that they

understood what she had done, and they raised a tomb unto her, and thenceforward all the youths and maids of Telmaris came to the edge of the sea, to the shrine of Phile, and did honour to her there.

THE TWO S.S.

THE TWO S.S.

THEY were hot in discussion, and the fair boy, with all the ardour of youth, strode about the room, and in poetical language pushed his arguments and hurled his epithets with infinite determination and conviction against the elder man, who, albeit he grew hot at times, was on the whole more quiet, speaking, if with less heart, with more reason.

Particularly interesting was the manner in which each embodied the spirit of his respective cause in the form of a personal creature of goodness and beneficence, disinterestedly striding over the world with a hand outstretched to help and purify humanity, whilst describing that of his adversary as an undoubted evil to be crushed with no quarter.

The youth alluded to the depraved and selfish monster who, through greed of impotent knowledge, tortured the suffering. Whilst the other received "impotent" with a sneer, and described sentimentality and personal fear of suffering as the basis of all evil, which deterred progress and prevented the alleviation of the pain of countless thousands in the future by an hysterical horror of inflicting any kind of immediate suffering.

The discussion was started on the question of Science and Sentiment. I became half mesmerised by the continuous flow of words, which promised little variation at last, and closed my eyes.

When I opened them, seemingly, a half minute later, the noise of talk had died; I found myself in a great meadow where sat, not far from me, two little girls, and, strangely enough, I found I could understand their innermost thoughts even as if I were of them, and one seemed to be the child of Science and the other of Sentiment, and their names were Luzia and Estrith.

They sat, these two little creatures, on the grass, which sloped down to a full stream, then rose again up to the confines of a dense fir wood which was as a black line on the horizon dividing the green from the intense blue of a summer sunlit sky.

There was something of the fair meadow and luminous heavens in the countenance of the one, whilst that of the other, a strange, elfish little person with pale face and dusky hair, suggested the wood beyond of· impenetrable shadow. Her unchildish hands were narrow and with pointed fingers, and her countenance quite serious. She held a fly in her hand, and was deeply interested in its movements, threatening to disembarrass the poor crawling creature of its wings, and quite indifferent to the pressing protestations of her companion, who was not to be persuaded to take part in the operation, even for the promised delight of " seeing what would happen."

The latter was the younger of the two, and, in spite of her opposition, seemed to be in some awe of her playmate. She spoke with a certain beseeching humbleness—she would pay homage, even though the fly were tortured ; but until then she would continue the fight to save it. The inevitable quarrel ensued ; the fly lost its wings, and the little person—such a tiny little girl—who wanted to see what would happen, forgot her interest and walked solemnly away.

Estrith sat quite still—the tears slowly crept into her eyes and coursed down her cheeks, whilst Luzia hovered apart, pulling flowers and humming a little song. The diswinged fly crawled unhappily on the ground between them.

Some time passed in this manner, till the little maid gathering flowers suddenly cast them down and proceeded to amuse herself by solemnly rolling down the grassy steep. The other, equally solemn, watched her go through this performance several times and gradually grew fascinated.

Rolling was irresistible ; she forgot her tears and her fly and fell to doing likewise. Down they went, these two, over and over, still without a smile, when at last a very jerky, unexpected bound started a laugh, and therewith the quarrel was obliterated. They raced each other to the top only to fling themselves down again, pressing the long grass flat with their warm little bodies, and shouting at the top of their tiny voices as they came dangerously near side by side.

The gleaming golden curls were in close proximity to the little black head. Collision was imminent, and when it came they received the shock with a redoubled shout of hilarity.

To tumble over one another seemed

wonderful sport, and then, in the midst of such a moment, a thin little hand stretched out and pulled vigorously at the yellow mesh of hair. Immediately they both sat up, flushed and rough-headed.

"What did you do that for?" queried the offended one.

"Pooh!" said the other, "to see if it would hurt."

The perfect calmness of this reply was peculiarly stinging, so that the tears started afresh into the baby's eyes, whilst the elfish Luzia looked oddly at her for a moment, then danced off after a butterfly, with an expression on her face of absolute scorn for one who would cry at so little provocation; and after flitting about, one moment in a broad flood of sunshine, then in the blue shadowy places, pursuing the butterflies with unabated energy, she returned, her hat in her hand, carefully covered with a large leaf to prevent the escape of two yellow-winged little prisoners ; and, ignoring the fact that Estrith was still very doleful, she commanded her amicably to take care of "the capture." Undoubtedly Luzia was conscious of her power, for she was obeyed with alacrity, and the charge was accepted with evident pride at so much confidence shown. Consequently, the little huntswoman departed again in hot pursuit.

She seemed a long time away to the wistful keeper, who, so long as her companion remained in sight, was amply amused in watching her flit to and fro ; but upon her departure to an adjoining field the sunny-haired little girl found time begin to hang heavily indeed, and sought to amuse herself in vain ; then she gave a peep under the leaf. There they were, those poor imprisoned ones, beating their

wings sadly against the side of their
small cell! She wondered if they could
breathe there? And if they knew they
were doomed to be stuck on card-
board?

" Poor wee, wee butterflies!" she
chanted in an odd little voice, and covered
them again.

Still Luzia did not come, and the sound
of their flapping wings seemed to increase.
Perhaps they were very frightened. Perhaps a great big butterfly was waiting for
them on some flower. She peeped again.
The soft yellow powder from their bodies
stained the hat; she tossed off the leaf
angrily, but they seemed powerless to
move; she touched one with the tip of
her baby-finger, therewith they rose and
flew away, and she watched their flight
with the sweetest smile in the world on
her tiny face.

When they were quite gone and she glanced back at the empty hat she was frightened, and she waited with a brave little white face for the coming of her friend. She came, Luzia, and as she realised what had happened a flush of anger crept over her countenance, and then—which seemed to Estrith by far the worst to bear—an expression of contempt took possession of her whole demeanour, and she turned and walked away towards home.

The baby did not cry this time; she understood the other's displeasure, and was sorry that she had caused it, but she did not regret what she had done. She got up and toddled after her; the uneven steep was very difficult to descend, but she determined to bear the penalty for her disloyalty, only she thought about it in quite a different way.

They went some distance in this odd

fashion, the elder hurrying along heedless of the disgraced one following. The sun had set, and the world, from all its golden brightness, had turned into a pale, shadowy place, and the trees and grass seemed to shiver with the new cold breath rising up everywhere, and smiting, even as a damp hand, on the face. Cold, too, she felt, little Estrith, right down in her heart, and fright of the big bushes began to creep over her.

Then, suddenly, Luzia turned abruptly and walked straight back to the little one, just as she was stumbling over a stone, and took her hand in hers with a warm, firm grip. There was a sense to Estrith of wonderful protection in the touch of her hand : and indeed in the elfish, dark, little person there was a strange look of the maternal as she came back, when it was growing dusky, not as the offended playmate, but as the protector of the helpless, the mother to the child even though a little, child the mother !

*　　*　　*　　*

I stirred, and on looking up found my friends sitting silently, each with a look of perpetual implacability, and the demon of scorn in their eyes. " After all," I said, " you are both right. Science and Sentiment are sisters, and, hand in hand, they may shower beneficence wherever they go ; whilst, severed, one stumbles in the dark, and the other grows savage in destructive greed. Surely one built the great ship which was to bound the waves, and, it seems to me, the other inspired him who was to dare her command."

JOHAN AND KINA

JOHAN AND KINA

THE STORY OF A POET-CHILD

THE children sat round and listened to the words of the priest, who came but once in three months and taught them all the little they knew. He had, therefore, a great deal to say, and was relating, in simple words, the story of the "Passion" to these wild little creatures of the mountains, who lived in black huts clinging on the edge of the rugged steep, far apart from one another, so that a whole morning's walking divided them ; and, but for those few dwelling-places, the mountains stretched uninhabited and solitary far to the north, to the east, and to the west; only south in the plains, more distant than the eye could penetrate, were there signs of human habitations. They sat in a little circle on the verdant ground in a hollow on the hill, their bright, fair faces all uplifted, their baby-mouths open, and their eyes riveted, expectant, on the speaker.

He was old, with quite white hair; but something of the purity of childhood seemed still to linger about the sweet graveness of a face which dared to smile e'en when most serious.

He had nigh ended, saying: "He gave His life that God might turn His wrath from the evil-doer; Christ died on the cross because men had sinned——" when he was interrupted.

"What is 'sinned'?" said a little child.

The good priest hesitated : he glanced

106

from the faces of his children-listeners to
the mountain world around, to the im-
measurable skies which seemed to laugh
at change in their own changing aspects—
the figure of truth with her mantles of
disguising clouds, to the religious mind
a figure of immortality.

As he gazed the present grew dim,
whilst the past rose up—crowds of suc-
ceeding events inundating those lonely
giant mountains, which formed a setting
to the fantasy, even as they may have to
the reality, centuries before. "What is
sin?" And lo! the figure of Cain, with his
angered and jealousy-stricken features,
came before the quickened imagination of
the old man. Aye, the sin of jealousy ! . . . .
Yet he had loved his God seemingly over-
much! Then all the flood of iniquity
over long, long ages swept past. What
was this triumphant shriek of horror?

or was it the cry for God from the beast?
—the impotent demand for good, giving
expression, because impotent, to evil which
mothered again Virtue—then should
heaven be born of hell! .... A moment's
dream, rising in the still hills and dying
there—a breath of wind laden with un-
seeming philosophy; and he answered
serene again from such unwonted medita-
tion, safe within the portals of orthodoxy:
"Sin is what a man doeth, knowing that
that which he doeth is wrong, and hurtful
to his brother or harmful to a fellow-
creature, though it be but a mule of burden
or e'en an enemy. .... And it was in those
times that men fought as beasts, and killed
one another, as your father might kill
the wild chamois, and God was angered
against them, and only the death of
Christ on the cross would turn His anger
into the channel of mercy."

Then the good Father rose and bid them get up and walk down a little of the way with him.

And the spell of seriousness broke at the sound of the changed tone, and they scrambled to their feet, half tumbling over one another, like a medley of flowers taking wing. They clustered about the priest; one held either hand, and several clutched his long black gown, hazarding his very life at every step, dangerous pioneers that they were! But there was a laugh at a slip, and tiny voices echoed about the silent world like the clinking of silver bells.

All the time of the lesson Johan and Kina had sat wistful and intent, hand in hand, with some shyness of the other children, whom they knew not well. So alike were these two that the little girl seemed only the bright reflection of the grave boy, whose eyes had never reverted for one moment from those of the speaker. On rising, neither of them laughed as the others did, and they followed some way behind the train of babbling ones down the hill. Midway they halted and stood staring at the retreating procession, which gradually diminished as now and then some child dropped apart to take a particular footway home. When the priest was quite alone, a black figure in the world-wide spread of green, he turned to wave a hand at those higher up diverging on their several ways, and he caught sight of Johan and Kina—tiny creatures, dusky crowned, gazing solemnly after him with wide eyes, as the chamois looks, unfrightened yet by the hunter. He waved an extra "Good-bye," and a faint sweet look of acceptance spread over their faces as they shyly returned the salute.

Then these strange little persons scampered home, hand in hand, their brown wee feet beating on the hardened turf of the natural terrace, which widened out at last into the loveliest of all lovely places—a valley high up in the mountains, verdant as only such valleys are, with, deep in its very heart, a white quick-running stream.

A great crucifix stood in the open, and as Johan and Kina passed they slackened pace, and both the little heads turned upwards, and their eyes rested on the Christ the aged priest had told them of. Then they scrambled up the precipitous way to the higher level, where a sombre cottage clung to the very face of the rugged steep.

They entered into the low-roofed hut, and ran, laughing, to a great big peasant with dark beard and tanned countenance, and in the beautiful dialect of the hills

poured out their quaint talk. He continued
eating, not heeding them much; only now
and then his white teeth gleamed as some
babble fell more winsome, and this sign
was full happiness to them, and they
gobbled up their pottage like little
hungry animals, dispensing quickly enough
with the necessity of a meal. Mothered
by the big peasant only, they were quite
unused to softness; but the love-bond
was strong between them, even as the
sunlight between heaven and earth, and
the clinging of the reaching skies to their
own mountain peaks. Johan eyed the big
gun over the fireplace as he ate. Then
the three cleared the things away, and the
man came out, stooping as he emerged
from the low door, and sat on the wooden
steps, and Johan and Kina sat a little
way off, and Kina chanted into the ear of
a big daffodil, which raised its head high

above the waving grass; whilst Johan watched the smoke curl out of the peasant's pipe, and in the light clouds which hovered in the heavy atmosphere he fashioned the scenes of the story of Christ, the words of which echoed still in his ears from the morning; and at last he grew sleepy, and the head of the black bearded father became the crowned God on the cross.

*   *   *   *

One early morning, a full year later, when autumn was speeding again to winter, and the first snows were threatening to chase the shepherds to the lower valleys, where war was waging, Johan, breathless and half-clad, called:

"Kina! the great gun is gone from over the chimney!"

"Aye, Johan!"

" Kina, our father is killing men, even
as he killeth the chamois ! "

Then Kina sat up in the deep shadow
of her bed and peeped out at Johan
as he stood, pale, with the look of storm-
lit heavens in his grey eyes, and her fair
little face reflected the horror in his.

" No, Johan ! it is not true ? "

" Yea, Kina ; for I looked out over the
valley, and father was there, and they were
shooting ; and I looked to see the horned
creatures—but, Kina, they were men ! "

Kina slipped out of bed, and, going
to where he stood, took hold of his hand.
They knew nothing, these two little
persons, of war—nothing of how a hand-
ful of grown men called kings, or Govern-
ments, inveigled the poor of the land to
slay one another that their disputes might
be decided—the disputes of these masters
who sat and watched the flow of blood from

afar and cried exultant: "Mine where the stream runs thickest! Victory!"

And the blood too, O ye kings!

These children of the mountains guessed only that their father was sinning even as they sinned for whom the "Man" had died—that King crowned on the cross—on the big wooden cross without, and the terror of the thought made pale their childish faces.* The priest had said that only by Christ's death were those others forgiven. Who, then, would save their father? Christ was not there— no one to die for him!

* It should be noted here that the unusual horror Johan experiences at the thought of the sin of causing death is a particular instance arising out of the explanation given of sin to a poetically-minded peasant child, living with the only companionship of a little sister and a taciturn father; and serves to illustrate the extreme intensity of child faith.

"Kina!" said the boy after a pause : "God cannot pardon our father!" and he tightened his brown fingers over hers. Then, hand in hand, they ran out down the steep to the open. The world lay in the all-pervading whiteness of the hour claimed neither by night nor day. Grey and shadowy, the mountains seemed unreal, and the earth as nothing, and the heavens vast and infinite. Space had become conscious and breathing, and men as crawling phantoms. The quick sound of firing re-echoed though the air, and the peasants hurried ever to a new ambush, disorganised, defeated, yet determined e'en to death. They reached the Calvary, in the midst of the firing, Johan and Kina, unconscious of danger, and knelt down, and thought of all the prayers they knew, and said them one after another in haste, as if time were short for God to hear them—two little brown figures hardly visible a few yards distant.

A stray shot cut the air where the little girl knelt and splintered the wood of the cross. Johan ceased praying, and looked oddly at the place.

Then a strange thought crept in, and took possession midst the distraught confusion of his mind. He drew Kina from where she was, and knelt closer himself, and there was a look on his face as of one waiting.

How long a time passed before that great lull he heeded not, but the sound of Kina's voice had ceased with the firing, and the snow was falling thickly about. A sudden horror of the still silence gripped the boy, and, with a sense of uncontrollable fear leaping in his heart, he turned his head slowly round:

" Kina ! "

But she answered not : her little body lay across the steps of the Calvary, face downward and silent.

" Kina, it's all right—they are not fighting any more ! " he cried, and tugged at her gown ; then he lifted her head. " Kina ! Kina ! " he cried, louder and louder; but the echo of his voice beat back on his ears, and still Kina was silent.

He sat a long time near, brushing the snow away which kept piling up about her. He watched pathetically her face, as one hardly conscious of what had happened ; then dawned over his child-countenance a wondrous look of understanding : " Kina, *thou* hast done it ! " he said, as if she might hear him. " God will forgive our father now ! "

Therewith he sprang up and ran home.

God would forgive his father ! God would forgive his father !—over and over again the thought whirred in his poor little head, and the look of horror had passed ; but as he neared the hut he perceived two men, who bore a burden between them, approaching. He stood still, unnoticed, and they entered into his home, and came out ; and when they came out their hands were free, and one said : "The war is ended, but not our woe !" And the other answered : "God curse the tyrant !" And they went their way.

Johan for a moment hesitated, then ran in. Stretched on the bed lay his father, white, with a fixed gaze ; and he knew they had slain him, and the tears welled up into his eyes, and he shivered where he stood. The look of the dead man frightened him, for there was the stain

of blood on his face; the teeth gleamed
through the parting lips as if in anger,
and the silence of the cottage was round
him, and Johan was quite alone, and the
snow still fell without. Then he crept
out of the house and back the way he
had come, and as white as the snow was
his face, and the snow was not whiter
than his face.

But lo! when he came to the Calvary,
Kina was not there; only, resting in her
place, was the figure of a winged man—
a still angel!

*   *   *   *

The good priest climbed slowly up
the mountain-path with such things in a
satchel as might be needful to the wounded
peasants, who, at the end of the war,
had made this sudden, unpremeditated
resistance, rushing from their huts with
rage in their hearts and death in their

eyes, to fall, surely, before the trained arms-men of the oppressor.

It had been but a light skirmish up here in the heights, and quiet had taken her place quickly again in this early morning. The snow had fallen unremittingly, the snow, which was to remain the whole winter through, covering all with its white hand, and levelling the way about. Clouds covered the distant peaks, and the whiteness and the silence dazed the old man, fatigued from long administration. He rested a while in the valley, where stood the great cross. And, as he pondered, he saw a strange little figure, half-clad, kneeling there with upraised face and outstretched hand.

" Kina, Kina, I have come back ! "

Then full and perfect sounded the words from One unseen :

" She is not here. She is risen ! "

JOHAN AND KINA

And the boy got up slowly and came towards him like a maimed creature, no recognition in his wild eyes.

*   *   *   *

The Sceptic murmurs: "The aged priest had mistaken the voice of the wind! The angel was but the figment of a child-poet's mind! And the snow, in her shroud, had only covered up the dead Kina!"

*   *   *   *

That which we truly believe *is*.

Printed by BALLANTYNE, HANSON & CO.
London & Edinburgh